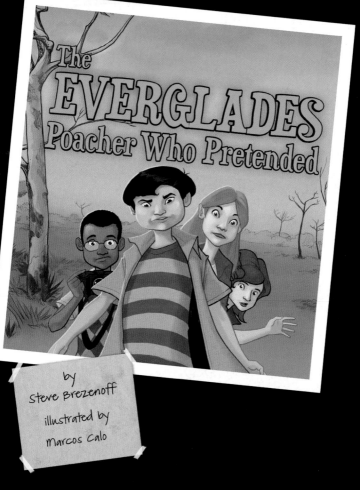

The EVERGLADES Poacher Who Pretended

by
Steve Brezenoff

illustrated by
Marcos Calo

STONE ARCH BOOKS
a capstone imprint

r Samantha Archer,

Field Trip Mysteries are published by Stone Arch Books
A Capstone Imprint
1710 Roe Crest Drive
North Mankato, Minnesota 55603
www.capstonepub.com

Library of Congress Cataloging-in-Publication Data
Brezenoff, Steven.
    The Everglades poacher who pretended / by Steve Brezenoff ;
illustrated by Marcos Calo.
        p. cm. -- (Field trip mysteries)
    ISBN 978-1-4342-3790-3 (library binding) -- ISBN 978-1-4342-
4197-9 (pbk.)
    1. School field trips--Juvenile fiction. 2. Poaching-
-Juvenile fiction. 3. Everglades National Park (Fla.)-
-Juvenile fiction. [1. School field trips--Fiction. 2.
Poaching--Fiction. 3. Mystery and detective stories. 4.
Everglades National Park (Fla.)--Fiction.] I. Calo, Marcos,
ill. II. Title. III. Series: Brezenoff, Steven. Field trip
mysteries.
    PZ7.B7576Eve 2012   2011053514
    813.6--dc23

Graphic Designer: Kay Fraser

Summary: While their sixth-grade class is on
a field trip to Everglades National Park, James
"Gum" Shoo and his friends find a suspicious
park ranger and a gang of poachers.

Printed in the United States of America in
Stevens Point, Wisconsin.
032012   006678WZF12

TABLE OF CONTENTS

James Shoo

A.K.A: Gum

D.O.B: November 19th

POSITION: 6th Grade

Is this because he chews a lot of gum?

INTERESTS:

Gum-chewing, field trips, and showing everyone what a crook Anton Gutman is.

KNOWN ASSOCIATES:

Archer, Samantha; Duran, Catalina; and Garrison, Edward.

NOTES:

Mr. Spade has made an effort to st... James from chewing gum in class. W... fear he cannot be stopped.

CHAPTER ONE

HOT

"Wow," Samantha said as we stepped off the bus. She put down her luggage on the pavement. Then she took off her silly old hat and fanned her face with it. "Too hot."

I followed her off, with Edward — that's Egg to you — and Catalina, or Cat, behind me. All of us had our luggage.

Sam was right. It was way too hot: muggy, sticky, humid, and hot, hot, hot.

"Stop!" I said.

Egg bumped into me on the bus steps, and Cat bumped into him.

"What are you doing, Gum?" Egg asked. He gave me a shove, but I didn't budge. I'm a lot bigger than Egg.

"I'm staying on the bus," I said, turning around. "It has air-conditioning." It was a great bus, too. This wasn't your typical school bus, or even a relatively fancy city bus. This was a top-of-the-line charter bus, with cushy seats, TV screens for every seat, and a big clean bathroom at the back.

I could have lived on that bus, as long it was parked near a diner.

Egg and Cat rolled their eyes, but that didn't stop me. Unfortunately, Mr. Spade, our sixth-grade teacher, was right behind them. He stopped me.

"Sorry, James," he said. "The bus will be going back to the depot now. It will be back to pick us up at five o'clock."

I let my shoulders sag. "Can't I go back to the depot too?" I said.

"Um, no," Mr. Spade said.

I looked past Mr. Spade at the bus driver, Gary. "I can hang out with Gary!" I said. My eyes got wide. "I bet he knows all the cool places to hang out in Homestead!" That was the nearest big town, east of Everglades National Park.

Gary laughed, but he shook his head. "Sorry, kid," he said. "I have a lot more jobs to do between now and five o'clock. There's a group of seniors to pick up and drop at the race track. Then there's the nuns playing bingo today. . . ."

He probably would have gone on, but Mr. Spade cut him off. "That's enough, James," he said. "Now turn around and disembark."

I cocked my head to one side. "Huh?" I said.

"That means get off the bus," Egg said.

"Darn," I said, but I turned around and climbed off.

Sam was still standing there, fanning herself with her hat. Once Egg and Cat were standing with us, Sam said, "Here we go again. Another field trip."

We all nodded, and Sam went on. "It's really too hot," she said. "I wish we could have come in the winter. Then it would be nice to be hot."

We watched the bus door close and the bus drive off.

"Well," I said, "hopefully this time we can just enjoy the field trip. I can't think clearly in this heat. A mystery is the last thing I need."

My friends agreed. Together, we followed Mr. Spade as he gathered together the rest of the sixth-grade class.

"What about our bags?" Egg asked. He thumbed over his shoulder at all the suitcases and duffels in the parking lot.

"Your bags?" Mr. Spade said. "Wait a second. Why did everyone unload their bags?"

"Gary told us to," I said. "I guess he needs the space for the rest of his driving jobs today."

Mr. Spade put his hands on his hips. He opened his mouth to talk. But just as he did, the sky seemed to crack open. There was a loud bang, and then another.

Mr. Spade threw his arms up and shouted, "Gunshots!"

Everyone dove onto the ground, which was very unpleasant, because the ground was very wet.

Well, not everyone dove onto the ground. When the shots stopped, I lifted my head and looked around. The park ranger was still standing, looking down at the sixth-grade class from Franklin Middle School, and our teacher.

"They must raise 'em pretty skittish back home, huh?" the ranger said. She was a young woman in green pants, a tan shirt, and one of those goofy ranger hats. She also had on sunglasses and a very grumpy expression.

Mr. Spade looked up at her. Then he got to his feet and brushed off the front of his shirt and tie. "Um, yes," he said. "Are there frequently gunshots in the park?"

The ranger used her index finger to push her hat back a little. I noticed out of the corner of my eye that Sam immediately copied the move. I guess looking cool in a hat takes some practice.

"More than I'd like," the ranger said. "Every time I hear a gun go off, it means some poor croc or turtle is about to turn into a pair of a shoes and an expensive steak."

Uh-oh, I thought. Cat was standing right next to me.

"What?!" Cat shrieked. Her voice trembled. "Turtle steak?"

"That's right," the ranger said. "There's a market for it, but the turtles in this park are an endangered species, so it's a crime."

Cat crossed her arms and clenched her mouth up so tight that her lips turned white. Egg patted her back.

The ranger pulled off her sunglasses. It was a smooth and quick move. "I'm Ranger Chavez," she said.

She slowly turned her head as we all stood up, and I swear she made eye contact with each and every sixth grader. I heard a few people gulp with fear. She was pretty scary, all right.

"Y'all can call me Ranger Chavez," she said. She gave us another sweep with her death glare.

"Well, thank you, Ranger Chavez," Mr. Spade said. "What should we do with our bags?"

Ranger Chavez snapped her fingers. Two younger park employees ran over to the bags and stood there. "They will guard the bags," the ranger said.

"She's tough," Sam whispered. "I like her." Cat nodded, dumbstruck.

"Now," Ranger Chavez went on, "here are some park rules." She started to walk off and was nearly twenty yards away before we realized we were supposed to follow her. Even Mr. Spade ran to catch up.

"No alcohol," Ranger Chavez said. I don't think she noticed the thirty sixth-graders running to catch up — or the forty-year-old man out of breath right behind her.

She kept rattling off the rules: no glass bottles, no guns, no motorized vehicles — including boats.

"You're going to look for the big, noisy, manatee-killing airboats," she snapped. "Everyone does. They're not here. They're illegal. So don't ask."

She went on like that for the whole walk down a sandy trail toward the river of grass — that's what some people call the Everglades. Mr. Spade taught us that on the bus.

The point is, Ranger Chavez had a long list of rules.

She finally stopped walking, right at the edge of the water, where a bunch of canoes were parked. Then she turned around and pulled off her sunglasses again.

I popped a bubble. She practically snapped her neck to glare at me.

Squinting, she held my eyes. I gulped in fear again. Then she said, "No gum chewing." Then she snarled. I swear.

SWALLOW YOUR GUM

"Swallow your gum," Egg whispered, quietly but urgently. "Swallow it before she reaches into your mouth and tears it out. She'll probably take your tongue and half your teeth with it!"

"I'm trying!" I said. It's hard to swallow three pieces of gum all at once, especially when your mouth is dry with terror. I had to bite it into smaller pieces first, and then swallow them one after the other.

Believe me, it was hard to concentrate with the Warrior of the Everglades, also known as Ranger Chavez, walking toward me. Her face was getting redder and redder.

I worked the gum in my mouth, trying to swallow it bit by bit. I finally got the last lump down my throat when she was two steps away. By the time she reached me — and stood with her face only inches from mine — I could hardly breathe. Somehow I managed to smile.

"Open," she said, or grunted, "your mouth."

So I did, still smiling. "Ahh!" I said. "No cavities!"

A few kids laughed, but Egg just covered his eyes and shook his head. He worries too much.

The ranger stood up straight and stared me down. I kept smiling. Before long, my face hurt, and I wanted some more gum.

"This time," the ranger said quietly, so only I could hear her, "you're lucky. If I see your jaw working again and there's no words coming out of your mouth . . ."

She pulled her first finger across her throat. "Got it?" she said.

I stopped smiling and nodded vigorously. "I got it," I said.

She leaned closer to me. "Got it, what?" she said.

"Got it, Ranger Chavez! Sir! Ma'am! Ranger!" I said.

I was glad it was so hot, because I would have been sweating under her stare even in the arctic.

"Good," she said. Then she went back to the head of the group.

"I don't think she likes me," I whispered to Egg. He just nodded.

"Okay, everyone!" Ranger Chavez shouted. "Grab a life jacket and pile on. We're going canoeing."

THIRD CANOER

In all, there were probably ten canoes: enough for three students and one grown-up in each.

Of course, that meant my friends and I had to split up, at least a little. To make sure none of us were on our own, we split up in pairs.

I went with Egg in one canoe, and Cat and Sam got into another one. That meant we'd each get assigned one more kid, and a grown-up chaperone.

I sat in the middle of our canoe, and Egg sat in the front. We each put on a bright-orange life vest.

I watched Sam and Cat climb aboard their canoe. They ended up with Henry Halper. He's a nice guy. And their grown-up was Henry's mom, the parent chaperone for the trip. So that wasn't too bad.

They were lucky.

Ranger Chavez climbed aboard our canoe. She sat in the back, and she put something on the floor of the canoe in front of her. It was covered with a heavy cloth, so I couldn't see what it was.

"I'll be watching you, gum chewer!" she called out.

I quickly faced forward.

And then it got worse.

When the canoe shook a moment later, I turned to see who was coming aboard.

Our third kid got on and pulled on his life vest. Then he turned to Ranger Chavez and said, in a sweet and sickening voice, "You're sure good at your job, Ranger Chavez. Gum here is the biggest troublemaker in our class." He was lying, obviously.

"Is that so?" Ranger Chavez asked, staring at me.

The boy nodded. "Yup," he said. "That's why Mr. Spade put me in this boat. He knew I'd keep an eye on him."

"In that case, I officially name you a temporary deputy ranger for this canoe trip," Ranger Chavez said. "What's your name?"

"Gutman," the boy said. He looked at me and smirked, so the ranger couldn't see him.

"Deputy Anton Gutman."

CHAPTER FIVE

DEPUTY GUTMAN

Anton Gutman is the sworn enemy of me and my friends, but especially me. I'll be the first to admit that whenever a crime is committed on a field trip, I point to Anton as my prime suspect.

Usually it's not him. But can you blame me? He's always starting trouble. He's always telling lies. He's always calling me and my friends names.

So there we were, starting a canoe trip through the Everglades that would probably last hours, and Anton was in our boat.

Worse, he was the official sidekick to the meanest, nastiest park ranger in the whole national park system.

"Pick up the pace up there!" Ranger Chavez shouted.

I guess my mind had been wandering. The other canoes had gotten pretty far ahead in the man-made canoeing lane through the grassy river. I turned around to say I was sorry, and I realized she and Anton weren't even paddling! Egg and I were doing all the work.

"This is some field trip," I grumbled to Egg. "We're the labor, and she sits back there, lounging with her new best friend, Anton the Deputy."

Egg was having a hard time too. Since he was so busy paddling, he couldn't take any photos.

Egg loves taking pictures. It's all he thinks about on field trips. And this was definitely a place where he'd want to take photos. There was super tall grass and funny-looking groves of trees growing right in the middle of the water! I also spotted some birds.

From pictures we'd seen in science class, I recognized a heron, an egret, and an osprey. I'm pretty sure I even saw a crocodile.

"It was probably an alligator," Anton said, after I shouted about the crocodile.

Ranger Chavez clucked her tongue. "Deputy Gutman is right," she said. "Alligators are far more common. Now pick up the pace."

Egg glanced at me over his shoulder from the front of the canoe. He was sweating a lot, and I was too.

From the look on his face, I could tell that he was also starting to think the worst of Ranger Chavez.

The ranger put a small bullhorn to her lips. "Attention, all canoes!" she shouted. I yelped. Right there in the canoe with her, it was deafening.

"Stop and head to the left-hand shore," the ranger bellowed through her megaphone.

Mr. Spade yelled back, "Okay!"

Ranger Chavez cleared her throat, with the megaphone still raised up to her lips. The sound rang out loudly across the river of grass.

"I mean," Mr. Spade shouted, "okay, Ranger Chavez!"

The ranger put down the megaphone.

"Okay, deputy," she said. "Help these two troublemakers steer the canoe to the left shore."

"When did I become a troublemaker too?" Egg whispered over his shoulder.

I shrugged. Then I struggled with my paddle to move us toward the shore.

"You heard Ranger Chavez," Anton said through a sneer. "Let's move it!"

I was glad she hadn't given him a whip. He probably would have used it, and Ranger Chavez probably would have cheered.

Before we reached the shore, Ranger Chavez stepped out of the canoe. I guess it was pretty shallow there. Plus she was wearing these big boots that went to her thighs. I noticed she left the covered bundle in the canoe, though.

She walked over to where the canoes had all stopped. Everyone was pulling their boats halfway onto a small island covered with plants and tall trees.

"This is a hammock," Ranger Chavez said as she reached the shore. She pulled off her sunglasses and spotted me. I was standing with Egg, and we'd found Sam and Cat pretty quick, too.

"And I don't mean a rope bed for lazy gum-chewers," the ranger said. Then she put her sunglasses back on. "Hammocks are the only dry land in the park," she went on, "besides the parking lot. Here you'll find several types of hardwood trees, and most of the animals that can't stay in water all day."

"What are some examples?" Mr. Spade asked. "Um, Ranger Chavez."

The ranger said, "There are deer, rabbits, frogs, snakes . . . they're all pretty elusive. I'm hoping we'll spot one of the most elusive — and rare — creatures in the park: the Florida panther."

At the very word "panther," the hairs on the back of my neck stood up. A chill ran up and down my spine and then up again. I shivered.

"You okay, Gum?" Sam asked. She snickered.

"Laugh if you want," I said. "But I don't plan on being eaten by a giant cat on this field trip."

"They won't eat anyone, Gum," Cat said. She put a hand on my shoulder. "Trust me, they're more afraid of you than you are of them."

"I think that's bears,"
Egg said.

I shook my head. "Couldn't be bears," I said. "Nothing could be more scared of anything than I am of bears."

"Good point," Egg said.

"Excuse me, Ranger Chavez?" I said politely. I raised my hand and everything.

"Yes?" she said through clenched teeth.

"Um, what should we do if we come across a panther?" I asked. "I mean, by accident, of course."

"It'll hear you coming," she said. "Look at it this way. If you manage to surprise a panther, I'd go play the lottery if I were you. You look like you'd have a hard time sneaking up on a log."

Anton thought that was hilarious. He nearly fell over laughing.

"But," Ranger Chavez said, "I intend to find a panther today, with you kids. It will be the thrill of your life."

She turned to start walking deeper onto the hammock. "Now," she said, "if you'll all follow me —"

But then a great crack burst across the small island. It was another gunshot, and this time it was closer.

"Stay here!" Ranger Chavez snapped at us.

The whole class — including the parent chaperones and Mr. Spade — snapped to frozen attention. Henry's mom even said, quite loudly, "Yes, Ranger Chavez!"

Henry tried to chuckle. "My mom was a Marine," he said.

The ranger ran into the deep growth of the island. Anton started to follow. Ranger Chavez stopped and spun to face him.

"What are you doing?" she snapped. "What part of 'stay here' did you not understand?"

Anton's face went white. "B-but," he said. "I'm your d-d-deputy."

The ranger looked confused for a moment. Then she burst out laughing. When she headed into the undergrowth, she was still laughing.

"I am not Anton's biggest fan," Sam said in my ear, "but that was just mean."

She was right. Even I had to admit it. Something about this ranger was not on the up and up. My friends and I would have to find out what.

"We have to follow her," Sam said.

The four of us slowly moved away from the main group. Soon after Ranger Chavez ran into the jungle-like island, everyone started talking excitedly. Even the grown-ups were pretty distracted.

"I agree," I said. "Gunshots, and the creepiest park ranger ever? Something's up."

"I don't know," Egg said. Now that we were safely on land, he was snapping loads of pictures in every direction. "Go into that crazy jungle? That doesn't sound safe."

"Egg might be right, guys," Cat said. She stood in front of me and looked right in my eyes. "Panthers," she said.

And there went the chills again, up and down my spine. I turned to Sam and said, "She makes a good point."

Sam sighed. "Three against one, huh?" she said, and we nodded. "Then I guess I'm on my own."

"What?" Egg said. He grabbed her wrist. "You can't follow her alone."

"Why not?" Sam asked.

"You don't know anything about this place," Cat pointed out. "What if you get a snakebite? Or even a bug bite!"

Sam tipped her hat back with one finger, just like Ranger Chavez had.

I rolled my eyes.

"If the ranger can do it," Sam said in a low, tough voice, "then I can do it."

"You can't go alone," Egg said. He took a step forward and added, "I'll go with you."

Cat and I must have looked surprised. In his glasses, V-neck sweater, and shiny brown shoes, Egg looked like the last guy who'd go gallivanting off into the jungle. Even in the right gear, he'd have a hard time keeping up with Sam. She's the fastest kid in sixth grade!

"I have the camera," Egg said. "And I know the most about the local animal population."

Cat shot him a look.

"Well, I scored the best on the test before the trip," Egg pointed out.

"By one point," Cat said. She crossed her arms. "I couldn't tell the difference between the Atlantic loggerhead and Atlantic hawksbill turtles."

Egg smiled. "See?" he said. "Let's go, Sam."

"Finally," Sam said with a huff. Then she took off into the woods. Egg hurried after her.

"This is crazy," Cat said. "What if they run into a panther . . . or an alligator?"

"I'm sure they'll be careful," I said.

I don't think Cat was really listening. She went on. "Besides," she said, "they'll never catch up to her."

"Maybe we can do some investigating from here," I said, glancing at the canoe we had arrived on. "Come on."

Cat and I walked over to the canoe. I could see the hidden bundle as we walked up. I tried to act natural.

"Aha!" Anton Gutman shouted. "What are you up to, troublemaker?" He ran over to me and Cat.

"Hello, Anton," I said.

"That's Deputy Gutman to you, Gummy Brain," Anton said. Then he shoved me to the side. "Now what are you two up to over here?"

Then Anton saw the bundle, too. "Did you put this here?" he asked. "Is it some kind of prank for the ranger?"

He got right in my face. His two goons, I noticed, had crept up behind me and Cat.

"We didn't put that there," I said. "It's Ranger Chavez's."

"Is that so?" Anton said. He started to lift up the cloth. I leaned forward to try to get a peek.

"Wait a minute," Anton said, letting go of the cloth. He looked at me and smiled. "Nice try, Gummy," he said. "You're trying to get me in trouble with the ranger. But it won't work."

He started to walk off. "Come on, guys," he said. His goons followed him, after grunting at me and Cat.

"That was lucky," Cat whispered.

I nodded. Then I knelt down next to the canoe. I reached out for the heavy cloth. "Let's see what the ranger is hiding," I said.

The moment my fingers touched the cloth, a shout came from behind me.

"Run!" Egg yelled.

I jumped up and faced the jungle. Egg and Sam came diving out of the undergrowth. Their eyes were wide with panic.

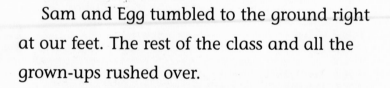

Sam and Egg tumbled to the ground right at our feet. The rest of the class and all the grown-ups rushed over.

"What is all the ruckus?" Mr. Spade asked.

"What were you two doing in the jungle?" Henry's mom asked.

Anton and his two goons stepped to the front of the crowd. "I'll handle this," Anton said. He added to Mr. Spade, "Ranger Chavez deputized me for this canoe trip."

Mr. Spade's mouth fell open, but he didn't reply. He probably couldn't reply. Anton was just that ridiculous.

"So, Archer," Anton said. That's Sam's last name.

Anton strode up to her, very confident. He wouldn't have been so confident without his two giant goons behind him, believe me.

"What exactly were you two dorks up to in there?" he asked. He nodded toward the interior of the island. "Were you spying on Ranger Chavez?"

Sam crossed her arms and stared him down. She didn't say anything.

Anton sneered. Then he turned to Egg. "Let me see that camera," Anton said.

"No way," Egg said, moving his body to shield his camera.

Anton elbowed one of his goons. "Take it," he said. "That's evidence that these two have been making trouble for the ranger. By the power vested in me —"

Just then, the ranger herself stepped out of the woods. She elbowed her way between Anton and my friends.

"Now," the ranger said, "time to get back on our canoes and shove off."

Mr. Spade stepped up to the ranger. "But we haven't even explored the island," he said.

"And we didn't get a look under that cloth!" I whispered to Sam.

"Did you two find anything out?" Cat asked Sam and Egg.

Egg lifted his camera to show us his newest photos. They were mostly pretty boring pictures of plants and the ground.

A few showed Ranger Chavez, stooping on the ground or looking at a branch.

"What is she doing?" Cat asked.

Sam said, "I figure she's looking for a poacher. She said poaching has been trouble for the park lately."

"I don't think a poacher would hide on a branch," I pointed out, "or under a leaf on the ground."

Egg laughed. "Tracks, silly," he said. "Sam means Ranger Chavez was looking for tracks."

I shrugged. "That makes sense, I guess," I said. "But what's so weird about that?"

The others shrugged too. By then, almost everyone else was on a canoe, so we climbed aboard ours, too. Maybe the ranger wasn't a criminal.

Maybe she was just
a mean ranger.

The next leg of the canoe trip started out pretty awful, just like the first. Anton and the ranger were best friends again. He started accusing me and Egg of trying to sabotage the canoe.

"Is that right?" the ranger said. She wasn't exactly surprised to hear the report. "I guess I didn't work them hard enough on the first leg."

She picked up her megaphone, put it to her lips, and shouted: "Row! Row! Row!"

Egg and I struggled and sweated. We were moving pretty quickly, if I do say so myself. But when another gunshot tore across the park, Ranger Chavez decided we weren't moving fast enough. "Time for the extra juice," she said.

I twisted my neck to see what she was doing. She whipped the cloth off the bundle in front of her, but I couldn't quite see it. Anton was in the way.

The ranger struggled with the bundle, her back to us. "Hold on!" she shouted. There was a great rumble, and the canoe shook. Then a grinding growl roared from the back of the canoe.

Then we shot across the river of grass like a speedboat.

NINE

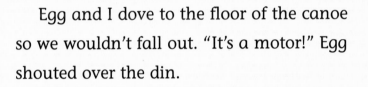

THIS WAY!

Egg and I dove to the floor of the canoe so we wouldn't fall out. "It's a motor!" Egg shouted over the din.

I nodded. "Yeah!" I said. "I figured that out, thanks!"

The ranger steered us right past all the other canoes. Before long, they were far behind us.

She ran us straight toward a hammock — one of those little, plant-covered islands.

The instant we were aground, the roaring motor stopped. Ranger Chavez stomped across the shallow water and onto the island.

"Stay here!" she commanded. Then she disappeared into the undergrowth.

I said to Egg, "Let's go."

"She said to stay here," Anton said. He stood on the shore with his arms crossed.

"We don't care what she said," I explained. "Egg and I want to know what's going on." With that, Egg and I headed deeper into the island.

"Wait up!" Anton shouted. Soon he was creeping along beside us.

"Just keep quiet," Egg said. His camera was to his eye, and he was snapping photos madly. I don't know why. All there was were plants and tree trunks. It was pretty boring.

"Which way did she go?" Anton asked.

I put out my arms to stop Egg and Anton. Then I got down on one knee and looked closely at the ground. There were footprints. Any fool could have found them.

"She went this way," I said, pointing at the path of footprints. They went straight ahead, and then curved to the left.

Egg took some photos of the prints. Then we hurried off after the ranger.

Before long, though, we reached the beach. The footprints ended at the shore — a different part from where the canoe was parked.

"Where'd she go?" Anton asked. "Did she swim away and leave us here?"

I think he was actually starting to panic. Some deputy.

"Let's get back to the canoe," I said.

"But what about the ranger?" Egg said. "The tracks end here."

I started back toward the other shore. "I wouldn't worry about that," I said. "Those weren't her tracks."

By the time we got back to the canoes, Ranger Chavez was already there. She got back into the canoe, took off the motor, and put it back under the cloth. For once, she looked pretty relaxed.

"Should we push off?" I asked.

"What?" Ranger Chavez said. "Oh, sure. Whatever."

Egg and I exchanged a glance. I was starting to think my latest theory was correct, but I couldn't share it with Egg yet. The ranger and Anton would definitely overhear.

Anton got onboard, and the ranger just sat there. Egg and I pushed the canoe till it started to float.

Then we hopped in as gracefully as we could, which wasn't very graceful. We both got pretty wet.

We started rowing, me and Egg. This time the ranger didn't shout. She just leaned back, with her hands folded behind her head.

"So, um," I said, "did you find a panther?"

"Nope," the ranger said.

"Did you catch the poacher?" I asked.

She pulled off her sunglasses and glared at me. "Just row," she said. "No more questions."

So I rowed. Before too long, we were with the other canoes again. Egg and I steered our canoe so we were next to Cat and Sam's.

Since Sam was in the middle position of her canoe, she was only a foot or so away from me. I was able to whisper to her.

"We have to hurry," I said. "Back to the parking lot."

"Already?" Sam said. "But Gary won't be back for hours."

I shook my head. "Gary's back already," I said. "But he won't be for long."

"What are you talking about?" Sam said. "Did you find something?"

"Tracks," I said. "Let's just say they weren't left by a panther."

Sam squinted at me. "You have to trust me," I said. I knew she would.

"Okay, you three," Sam called out to Cat, Henry, and Henry's mom. "How fast can you row?"

"Um," Henry's mom said. "Why do you ask?"

But Cat and Henry didn't even hesitate, and soon Sam's canoe was shooting back up the river, toward the parking lot. Egg and I followed.

"What are you doing?" Ranger Chavez shouted. "I didn't tell you to turn around!"

Anton looked at me and Egg. Then he shrugged and started to help.

"I hereby strip you of your title, former Deputy Gutman!" the ranger said.

But it didn't work. Anton paddled like crazy. And since he wasn't as tired as Egg or me, we picked up a lot of speed.

I spotted Gary's bus from the river.

"There he is!" I shouted, pointing at the parking lot. He was loading something into the luggage storage under the bus.

"Uh-oh," Ranger Chavez said. "What is he still doing here?"

We grounded the canoes. "Come on, Sam," I said. "You guys, keep an eye on the ranger."

Sam and I sprinted across the parking lot toward the bus. Gary spotted us and hurried to close the luggage compartment. He ran for the door, but Sam got there first and blocked his way.

"Hey, what's the idea?" Gary asked.

Sam smirked at him and crossed her arms.

A moment later, Mr. Spade, Cat, and Egg walked up. Ranger Chavez walked behind them, and Anton walked behind her.

"What's in the luggage compartments, Gary?" I asked.

"Why, luggage, of course," Gary said, laughing. "What else would be in there?"

"Whose luggage?" I asked. "The seniors at the race track? The nuns at the bingo hall?"

"Wh-what?" Gary stammered. "I . . ."

"Next time you should come up with some better fake jobs, Gary," I said. "Because I don't think they'd bring luggage. Is it our luggage?"

"Nope," Egg said. He pointed past the bus, where the two young park employees were still standing with our bags. "Our luggage is right where we left it."

Mr. Spade strode up to the one of the luggage compartments' door. He tried the handle.

"Locked," Mr. Spade said. "Hand over the key, Gary."

Gary closed his eyes and smirked. "No way," he said.

"I don't think we want to open that one," I said, walking up to the door. "Watch this."

I raised my fist, watching Gary. His smile fell as I slammed my fist against the metal door. Inside the compartment, something thrashed and roared. Claws scraped the inside of the compartment.

Ranger Chavez stomped past Mr. Spade and my friends, right up to Gary. "Why is it awake?" she snapped.

"I don't — I don't know!" Gary said. He backed up toward the bus door. "I did just what you told me!"

Mr. Spade's jaw dropped. "Ranger Chavez," he said. "You're the poacher?!"

"That's right," I said. "She and Gary are working together. She tracks the beasts, and Gary hauls them off."

"Then what do they do with them?" Henry's mom asked.

Cat cut me off when I tried to answer. "I'd rather not know," Cat said.

Henry's mom covered her mouth — like she might cry.

Mr. Spade called over the two young park employees to take Gary and Ranger Chavez into custody.

"But how did you know?" Egg asked.

"Simple," I replied. "First there was the luggage. I didn't think of anything of it right away, but then I realized something. A bunch of nuns playing bingo and a bunch of seniors betting on races wouldn't need luggage."

"So then why did we have to unload our bags?" Sam added, finishing my thought for me.

"Exactly," I said. "He needed the space to haul off their catch today. Then there were the gunshots."

"Poachers," Cat said. Then she snapped her fingers. "But the panther is fine. No one shot it. So what were the gunshots for?"

"A signal," I said. "Ranger Chavez had us paddling like mad, because she had to get to the signal to meet up with her contact."

"Gary," I said. "Egg, show me the photo you took on the second island. The one of the footprints."

Egg found the photo and held out the display for us to see.

"Two sets," I said. I pointed at the screen. "See? One has deep treads, and small feet. The other feet are very big, and the treads run diagonally. Those are Gary's shoes."

Mr. Spade nodded. "I see," he said. "Um, I think, anyway."

"Once I realized he'd been on the island," I went on, "and left quietly by boat, I knew they were working together."

Sam clapped me on the shoulder. "Good job, Gum Shoo," she said.

Anton stood there, shaking his head. "You can be the deputy next time," he said. "I'm done with the crime-fighting business."

literary news

MYSTERIOUS WRITER REVEALED!

Steve Brezenoff lives in St. Paul, Minnesota, with his wife, Beth, their son, Sam, and their small, smelly dog, Harry. Besides writing books, he enjoys playing video games, riding his bicycle, and helping middle-school students work on their writing skills. Steve's ideas almost always come to him in his dreams, so he does his best writing in his pajamas.

arts & entertainment

ARTIST IS KEY TO SOLVING MYSTERY, SAY POLICE

Marcos Calo lives happily in A Coruña, Spain, with his wife, Patricia (who is also an illustrator), and their daughter, Claudia. When Marcos and Patricia aren't drawing, they like to go on long walks by the sea. They also watch a lot of films and eat Nutella sandwiches. Yum!

A Detective's Dictionary

chaperone (SHAP-ur-ohn)–a person who looks after a group of people

deputy (DEP-yuh-tee)–a person who helps or acts for someone else

endangered (en-DAYN-jurd)–a species that is in danger of becoming extinct

evidence (EV-uh-duhnss)–information and facts that help prove something or make you believe that something is true

illegal (i-LEE-guhl)–against the law

poacher (POHCH-ur)–a person who hunts or fishes illegally on someone else's land

prime (PRIME)–main, number-one

ranger (RAYN-jur)–someone in charge of a park or forest

sabotage (SAB-uh-tahzh)–the deliberate damage or destruction of property

temporary (TEM-puh-rer-ee)–lasting only for a short time

theory (THEER-ee)–an idea or opinion based on facts but not proven

tread (TRED)–the ridges on the bottom of a shoe

Gum Shoo

Sixth Grade

(A)

The Everglades

The Florida Everglades are located in South Florida. They have been considered a national park since 1947, but the actual Everglades themselves have existed for thousands of years! Unfortunately, they are in trouble. When people wanted to build their homes in South Florida, they had to dry out the land first. That has endangered the Everglades ecosystem.

The Everglades are a large area of swamp, river, prairie, marsh, and hardwood hammocks in Florida. Some of the many animals that live in the Everglades are raccoons, turtles, alligators, manatees, vultures, and egrets. There are also many mosquitoes and butterflies and other insects.

efore the Everglades became a national park, many people thought that the land was just a worthless swamp. However, in 1947, a book called EVERGLADES: RIVER OF GRASS was published by a woman named Marjory Stoneman Douglas, a Florida journalist. Ms. Douglas worked to help restore the Everglades, and her book helped convince people that the Everglades were an amazing place. Today, people are still working to restore the Everglades. The project is scheduled to be completed in 2040.

Gum – Great essay. I hope we can go back in 2040 to see how things have changed! – Mr. N

FURTHER INVESTIGATIONS

CASE #FTM14GSENP

1. In this book, my class went on a field trip. What field trips have you gone on? Which one was your favorite, and why?

2. If you went on a field trip to the Everglades, what would you be most excited to see? Talk about your answer.

3. Who else could have been a suspect in this mystery?

IN YOUR OWN DETECTIVE'S NOTEBOOK . . .

1. Write about a time you couldn't trust an adult. What happened?

2. Sam, Cat, Gum, and Egg are best friends. Write about your best friend.

3. This book is a mystery story. Write your own mystery story!

THEY SOLVE CRIMES, CATCH CROOKS, CRACK CODES, ...AND RIDE THE BUS BACK TO SCHOOL AFTERWARD.

Meet Egg, Gum, Sam, and Cat.
Four sixth-grade detectives and best friends.
Wherever field trips take them, mysteries
aren't far behind!

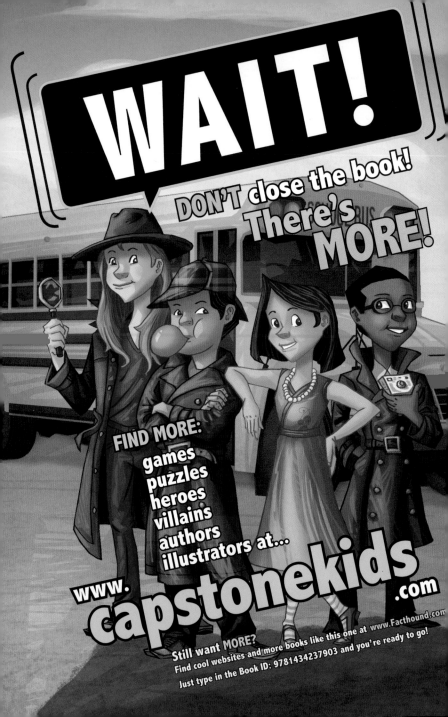